This book belongs to
Este libro pertenece a

_____

ISBN 979-8-9911153-0-8

Friends
Amigos

Alma Edith

Things to think about before reading.

Cosas para pensar antes de leer.

Do you have good friends?
¿Tienes buenos amigos?

Why are some friends mean?
¿Por qué algunos amigos son malos?

Why are some friends nice?
¿Por qué algunos amigos son amables?

Why are you a good friend?
¿Por qué eres un buen amigo?

A bad friend walks away from you.
Un mal amigo se aleja de ti.

A good friend doesn't hit or push you.

Un buen amigo no te golpea o te enpuja.

A bad friend will hurt you and make you cry.
Un mal amigo te hará daño y te hará llorar.

A good friend is nice to you.
Un buen amigo es amable contigo.

A bad friend is mean.
Un mal amigo es malo.

A good friend lets you borrow things when you need them.

Un buen amigo te presta las cosas cuando las necesitas.

A bad friend never lets you borrow anything.
Un mal amigo no te presta nada.

A good friend takes turns.
Un buen amigo se turna.

A bad friend always wants to be first.
Un mal amigo siempre quiere ser primero.

A good friend follows the rules of the game.
Un buen amigo sigue las reglas del juego.

I like playing with you because you always follow the rules.
Me gusta jugar contigo porque siempre sigues las reglas.

A bad friend cheats and says he wins, even when he doesn't.
Un mal amigo hace trampa y dice que ganó aun cuando no gana.

A good friend plays with you.

Un buen amigo juega contigo.

A good friend helps you.
Un buen amigo te ayuda.

A bad friend never wants to help you.

Un mal amigo nunca quiere ayudarte.

Good friends make your heart feel happy, like it is floating in the sky.
Un buen amigo hace que tu corazón se sienta feliz, como que flota en el cielo.

A bad friend
makes your
heart feel
sad, like if it is
falling to the
ground.
Un mal amigo
hace
que tu corazón
se sienta triste,
como si se
cayera al suelo.

The world is full of good friends.
El mundo está lleno de buenos amigos.

Some friends are
waiting to meet
you.
Algunos amigos
esperan conocerte.

What can you do if a friend is not being good to you?

¿Qué puedes hacer cuando un amigo no es bueno contigo?

Tell your friend what he or she is doing wrong.
Dile a tu amigo lo que está haciendo mal.

Problem solve with your friend and find a solution.
Resuelve el problema con tu amigo y encuentra una solución.

Find a better friend.
Encuentra un amigo que sea mejor.

Talk to an adult.
Habla con un adulto.

Remember, always
be a good friend
yourself!
¡Recuerda, siempre
sé un buen amigo!

What three things make a good friend?

¿Qué tres cosas hacen un buen amigo o amiga?

1.

2.

3.

www.ingramcontent.com/pod-product-compliance
Lightning Source LLC
Chambersburg PA
CBHW041007170626
46815CB00002B/198